I DON'T LIKE CHEESE

For Mr Holland — thank you for inspiring me to write this story.
And to my good friend Jordan — thank you for being such an
important part of this journey. — HC

Dedicated to the ones who bring me cups of tea and give me courage. — LM

First published 2014

EK Books
an imprint of Exisle Publishing Pty Ltd
'Moonrising', Narone Creek Road, Wollombi, NSW 2325, Australia
P.O. Box 60–490, Titirangi, Auckland 0642, New Zealand
www.ekbooks.com.au

A CiP record for this book is available from the National Library of Australia.

ISBN 978-1-921966-66-8

Designed by Big Cat Design
Typeset in Lemonade 23 on 35pt
Printed in Shenzhen, China, by Ink Asia

This book uses paper sourced under ISO 14001 guidelines from well-managed
forests and other controlled sources.

10 9 8 7 6 5 4 3 2 1

I DON'T LIKE CHEESE

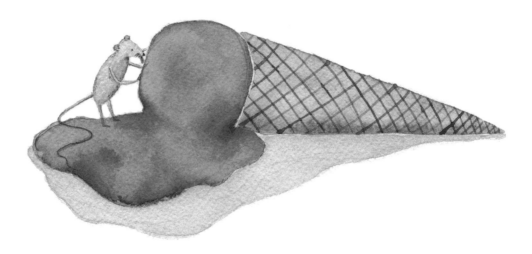

Hannah Chandler

Illustrated by Lauren Merrick

This house is home to the Walker family, but they're not the only family who lives here.

In the dining room there is a
mouse hole, and in that mouse
hole live Mike and his *mum*.

Mike wasn't always like other mice – he didn't like cheese!

It didn't matter what type
of cheese his mum gave him,
Mike refused to eat it.

Instead of eating cheese, Mike sat
patiently each night and waited for
the little girl of the house, Ashley, to
bring him something yummy for dinner.

Ashley always
left him a little
something to show
which country the
food came from.

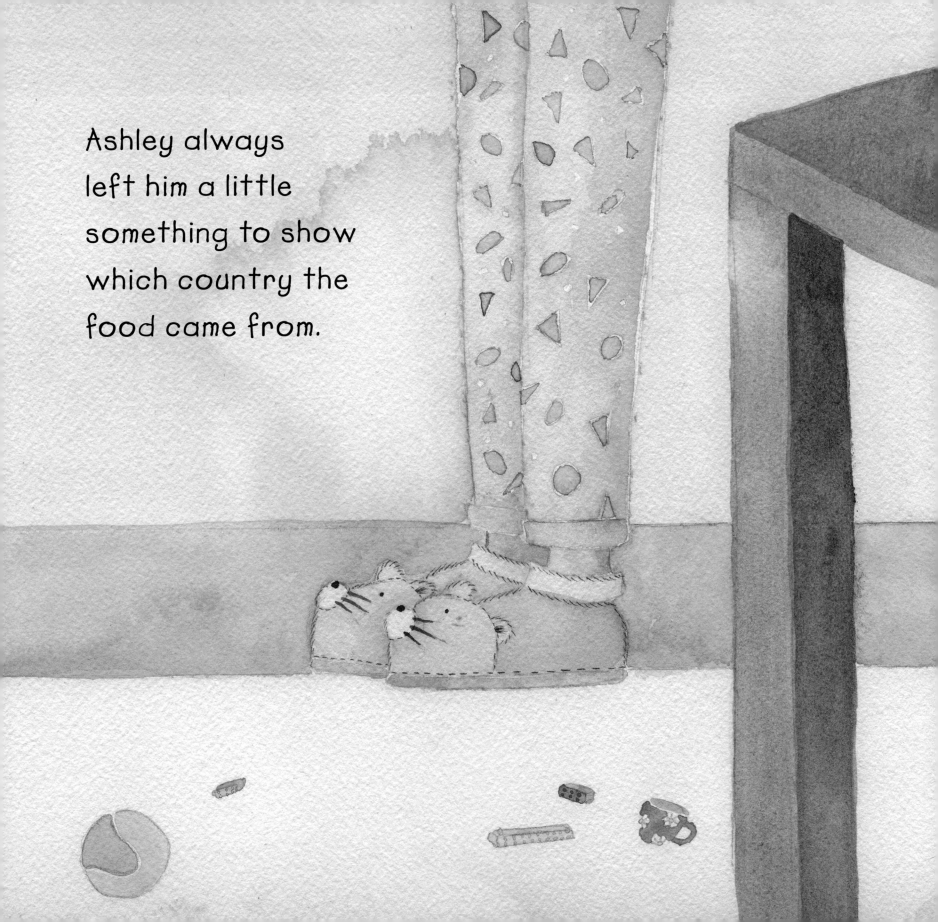

On Monday nights, Ashley
brought him a meat pie with
a good squirt of tomato sauce,
and lamingtons for dessert.
Ashley also brought him a little
cork hat to represent Australia.

On Tuesday nights, Mike tucked into tacos.
And Ashley gave Mike a sombrero to
show that tacos are Mexican.

On Wednesday nights, Mike enjoyed some sushi, and wore a cute little blue kimono from Japan.

On Thursdays, it was pizza night!
Pizza night was Mike's favourite
because he got gelato for dessert.

A little Italian flag showed that
pizza and gelato are both Italian.

On Fridays, Ashley served Mike croissants and a delicious crème brûlée for dessert, with a little French beret for him to wear.

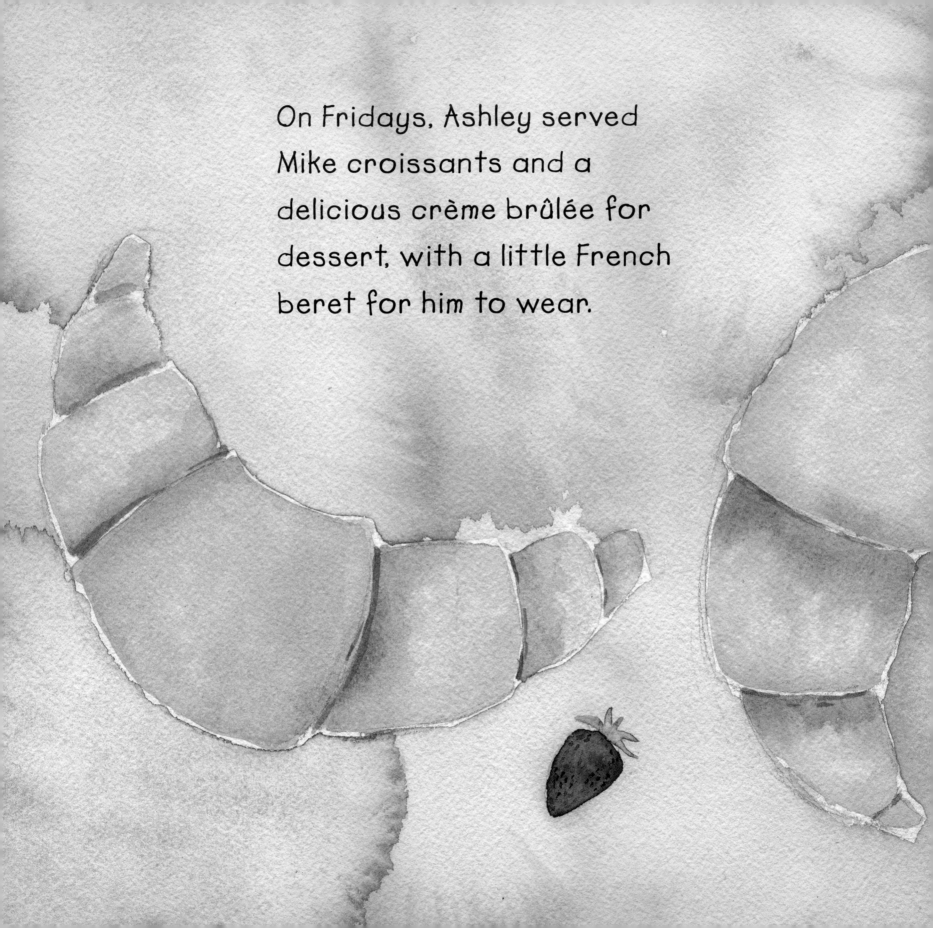

But one particular Friday, there was also a note on the tray for Mike:

To my little mouse friend,
My family and I are going on a holiday tomorrow.
Unfortunately, I will not be able to leave you dinner.
I am very sorry.
Love Ashley

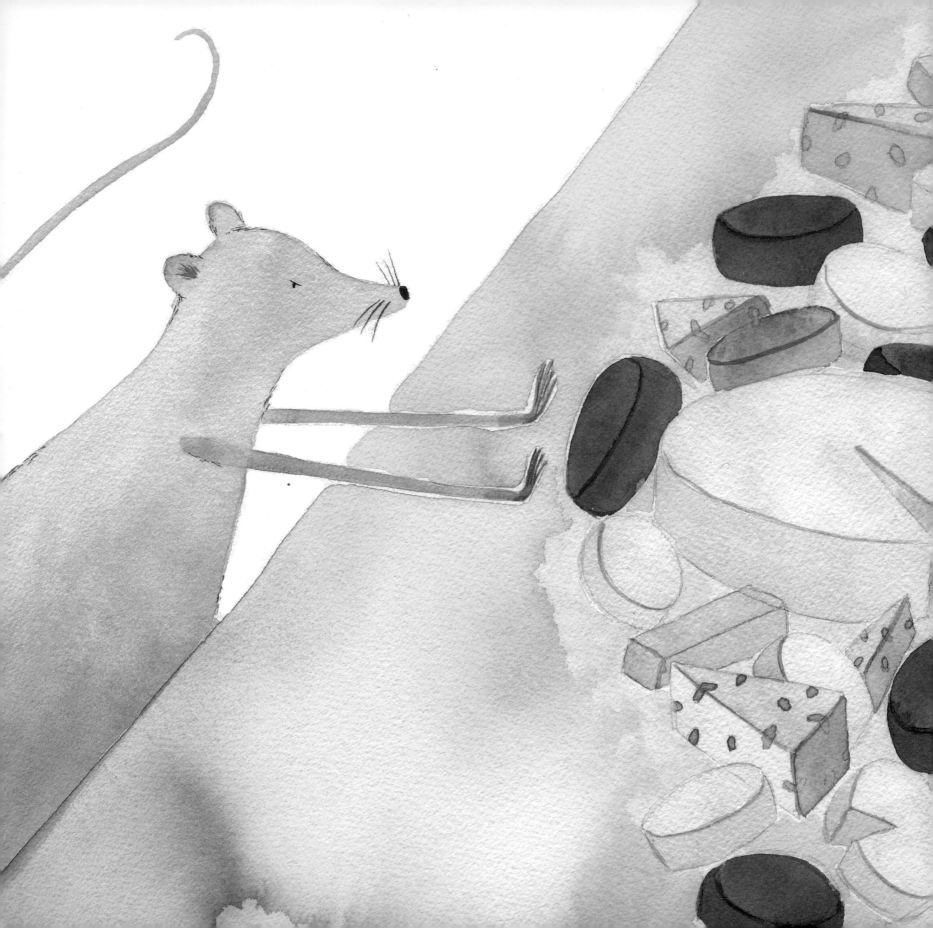

Mike refused to eat
anything that Saturday,
and pretty soon his little
tummy started to grumble.

On Sunday, Mike couldn't take it anymore, so his *mum made* him a delicious cheese platter. To his surprise, he LOVED it, especially the fancy cheeses like brie and camembert.

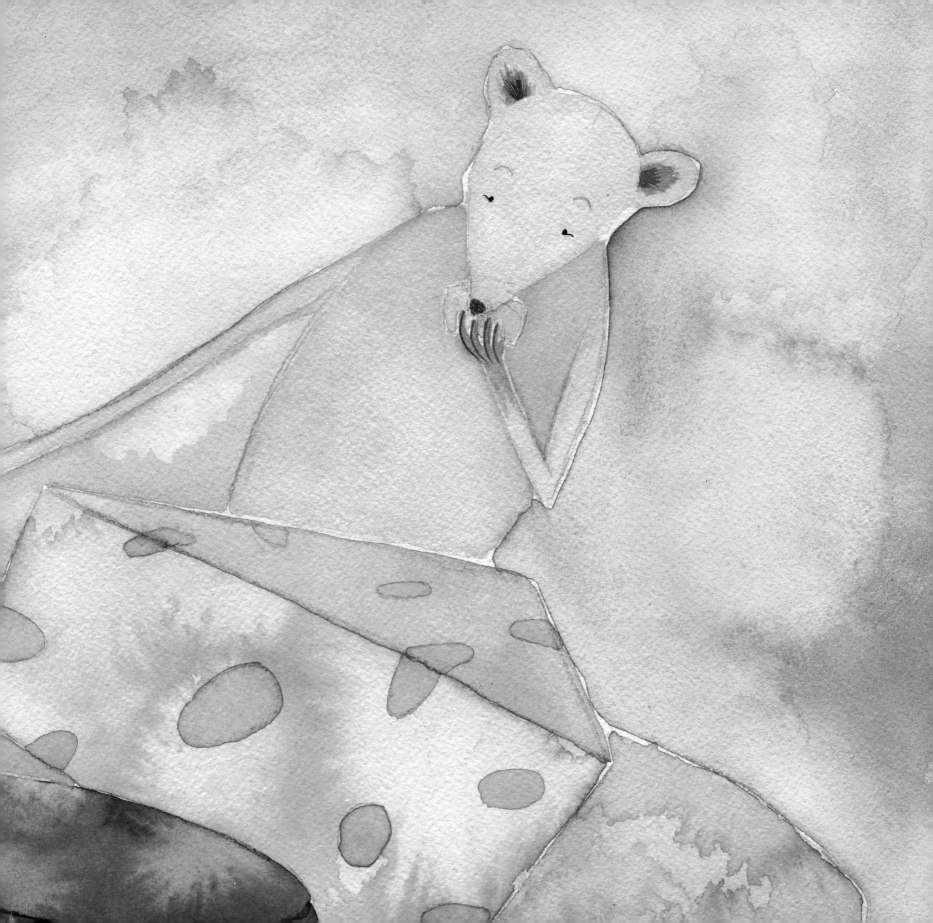

Suddenly Mike realised that quite a bit of the food Ashley gave him was made with cheese, so perhaps he did like cheese after all. In fact, it seemed he liked most food!

So Mike decided that from
then on he would eat the
cheese his *mum* gave him – but
still enjoy the occasional
treat from Ashley too!